CLASSIC FAIRY TALES

# Snow-White
## and
# Rose-Red

*Retold by Antonia Barber*
*Illustrated by Gilly Marklew*

MACDONALD YOUNG BOOKS

First published in Great Britain in 1997
by Macdonald Young Books
61 Western Road
Hove
East Sussex BN3 1JD

Text copyright © Antonia Barber 1997
Illustrations copyright © Gilly Marklew 1997

Designed by Shireen Nathoo Design

Typeset in 20pt Minion
Printed and bound in Belgium by Proost International Book Co.

British Library Cataloguing in Publication Data available.

ISBN:  0 7500 2025 3
ISBN:  0 7500 2026 1 (pb)

In a small clearing on the edge of a great forest, there once lived a poor widow and her two daughters. On the wall of their cottage grew a red rose and a white, whose scented blossoms tangled above the doorway. The girls were as sweet and as inseparable as the roses and so their mother called them Snow-White and Rose-Red. Though they

loved each other dearly, the two sisters were
very different. Snow-White was quiet and shy,
Rose-Red was brave and full of laughter.
Snow-White liked to work in the little cottage,

to see the floor swept and the kettle gleaming.
Rose-Red preferred the garden; she grew
vegetables and gathered flowers to make the
house bright.

In summer, when the days were long, the sisters wandered far into the great forest, picking berries and gathering wood, and no wild beast ever harmed them. When winter came and the snow lay deep over all the land, they lit their fire with the wood and made a warm cordial from the berries. Then, when darkness fell, they sat peacefully together in the firelight and the girls would spin while their mother read aloud to them.

One night, as they sat just so, there came a sudden loud knocking at the cottage door. Rose-Red sprang up and went to open it, thinking to find some poor traveller lost in the cold night. A flurry of snow blew in upon the keen wind and when it cleared she saw, beyond the doorway, the shape of a huge black bear. With a cry of fear, she ran back to her mother's side; the widow dropped her book and put her arms about her daughters.

But, to their astonishment, the bear spoke. "Have no fear," it said, "for I mean you no harm. Only let me warm my icy paws by your fire, for the cold freezes my very bones."

The widow saw that this was no ordinary bear: she rose and went to meet their strange visitor. Taking hold of his great paw with its claws like black icicles, she lead him towards the fire.

"You are welcome," she said. "Snow-White, warm up some cordial for our guest; Rose-Red, fetch the birch broom and brush the snow from his fur."

A little nervously, for he was a very large bear, the girls did as they were told. Soon the bear lay stretched out upon the hearth-rug,

warm and dry and in a very good humour.
Rose-Red began to comb the tangles from
his fur and then, growing bolder, plaited it
with red berries about his ears. The bear
seemed to enjoy this: he looked up at Snow-
White as if to see if she would join in the fun.

But Snow-White was shy; she sat at her
spinning wheel with her eyes cast down. When
she did glance up, she felt her heart beat
faster, for it seemed to her that she gazed not
into a bear's eyes, but into the eyes of a man.
At once the bear looked away, as if unwilling
that she should see into his soul.

All night long, the bear slept beside the fire. When morning came, he thanked them courteously, and went out into the cold forest. After that, he came every night and the door was never fastened until he was safe inside. For Rose-Red, he became a favourite pet. But Snow-White had looked deep into his eyes, and she knew, for all his fierce teeth and his sharp claws, that he was more than a tame bear. And Snow-White grew to love him.

When spring came, the snows melted and the forest grew green. The bear stood in the doorway one morning and sniffed the air. Then he turned to Snow-White and said, "I must leave you now and cannot return until winter comes again." His voice was low and Snow-White saw in his dark eyes a sadness at parting like the sorrow in her own heart. He turned away suddenly and, as he moved through the doorway, caught his fur against the iron latch. Snow-White cried out, expecting to see the red blood flow, but saw instead a gleam of gold under the dark fur. At once, the bear covered the rent with his huge paw and went swiftly away. Time passed and he did not come again.

One fine spring day, Snow-White and Rose-Red went out into the forest to collect wood. Coming upon a fallen tree, they saw a tiny dwarf whose long white beard was trapped in a crack of the wood. He scowled crossly at the two girls saying, "Don't just stand there! Come and set me free!"

Rose-Red tried to ease the wood apart, but it was too hard. "Useless creature!" snapped the dwarf. "Is that the best you can do?"

So Snow-White took from her pocket her little sewing scissors and snipped off the end of the long white beard. The little dwarf was free, but he was not at all grateful. "Wicked girl!" he cried, stamping his foot. "You have ruined my lovely beard!"

He reached into the hollow tree and pulled out a heavy sack that clinked as he threw it over his shoulder. Then, shaking his fist at them, he disappeared into the forest.

When high summer came, Snow-White and Rose-Red met the dwarf again. As they walked by the lake, they saw him leaping like a frog towards the deep water. "Help me!" he cried out. "Help me, you silly creatures, before I am drowned!"

They saw that his beard was caught up in his fishing line, and that some great fish

was pulling him into the lake. Just as he reached the water's edge, Snow-White took out the scissors and once again snipped through his beard. In so doing, she saved his life, but again he only cursed her for the damage she had done. Still grumbling, he reached down among the rushes and pulled up a net of pearls. He set them upon his shoulder, and stumped away through the trees.

The brown leaves of autumn had begun to fall before they saw the dwarf again. Crossing the open heath they heard cries of anguish overhead. Looking up, they saw an eagle clutching the ungrateful dwarf in his sharp talons. At once, Rose-Red climbed a high rock and as the great bird passed overhead, she caught hold of the dwarf by the hem of his coat. But the eagle was very powerful and would have carried her away too, if Snow-White had not seized hold of her sister's legs. Just as the coat began to tear under the strain, the eagle let go, and all three landed in a heap upon the ground. The dwarf was furious! "Just look at my coat!" he raged. "First you spoil my beard and now you have torn my fine coat!"

Snow-White and Rose-Red had grown used to his rudeness; they expected no better from him. They just smiled at one another,

and went on their way. But glancing back, they saw the dwarf take out a tin box from among the rocks and carry it into a cave nearby.

The shadows were lengthening as the two girls came home again, the rooks cawing noisily as they went to roost. Perhaps that was why the ungrateful dwarf did not

hear them coming. For as they passed the entrance to his cave, they saw how the setting sun gleamed upon a pile of gold coins, glowed upon a heap of fine pearls, sparkled upon a box of gems as the dwarf ran his fingers through them. Snow-White and Rose-Red gasped in astonishment. The little dwarf spun around and his rage knew no bounds.

"Three times I have spared you from my wrath," he screamed, "but this time you have gone too far! Because you have spied upon my treasures, I shall turn you both into a pair of toads!"

The girls were very frightened. What would their mother think if they did not return? But even as the evil little creature raised his hand to cast the spell, there came a loud roaring and a huge black bear rushed upon them.

The dwarf tried to escape into his dark cave, but the bear was there before him. Trapped, he began to plead, "Do not kill me, Bear! You shall have all my treasure if you will let me live." The bear growled angrily and moved towards him. "If you are hungry, Bear, I am but a scrawny creature; you will find these two plump young girls much tastier!"

At this, the bear roared as if in fury, then he struck the evil dwarf a blow with his great claws that silenced him forever. As he turned upon the two girls, Rose-Red drew back; but Snow-White reached out her hands to him and said softly, "Dear Bear, is it you?"

Even as she spoke, the rough bearskin fell away and before her stood a handsome young man. He smiled at her with the eyes she had grown to love, and taking her by the hand, told them both his strange story.

"I am a king's son," he said, "but my father grew old and ill, and our land became poor. I left the kingdom in the charge of my younger brother, and set out to seek a fortune and so save my people. After many adventures, I won this sack of gold, net of pearls and box of jewels. But as I took my way home, I fell foul of that greedy dwarf, who lived only for the treasure he could hoard in his dark cave.

Seeking to steal my riches, he turned me into a bear with a magic spell which could only be broken by his death. I fled with my treasures which I managed to hide. Through the cold winter my treasures were safe, for the frozen earth keeps the dwarves underground. When spring came, I knew that he would come seeking them. I hoped then to trap him and so break the spell. Three times I nearly caught him, but each time you set him free and he stole a part of my treasure."

"I fear we did you much wrong," said Snow-White.

The prince smiled. "Do you think I would love you less," he said, "because your hearts were kind?"

Then he took Snow-White in his arms and asked her to marry him and Snow-White said that she would.

Rose-Red kissed her sister joyfully, but there were tears in her eyes. "I thought," she said, "that we two should never be parted."

"Nor shall you be," said the prince. "You shall come with us to my kingdom and your good mother too. You gave me shelter when I was in need, and you shall all share in the good time that is to come."

There was such joy in that far kingdom when their prince returned with his rich treasure and his gentle bride. When Rose-Red met the prince's younger brother, they too fell in love, and both couples were married amid great rejoicing.

The good widow settled happily in a little house close by the royal palace. But first she planted two climbing roses, one on either side of the door. And one was snow white and the other rose red.

Other titles available in the Classic Fairy Tales series:

**Cinderella**
Retold by Adèle Geras    Illustrated by Gwen Tourret

**The Ugly Ducking**
Retold by Sally Grindley    Illustrated by Bert Kitchen

**Beauty and the Beast**
Retold by Philippa Pearce    Illustrated by James Mayhew

**Little Red Riding Hood**
Retold by Sam McBratney    Illustrated by Emma Chichester Clark

**Rapunzel**
Retold by James Reeves    Illustrated by Sophie Allsopp

**Jack and the Beanstalk**
Retold by Josephine Poole    Illustrated by Paul Hess

**Snow White and the Seven Dwarfs**
Retold by Jenny Koralek    Illustrated by Susan Scott

**Hansel and Gretel**
Retold by Joyce Dunbar    Illustrated by Ian Penney

**Thumbelina**
Retold by Jenny Nimmo    Illustrated by Phillida Gili

**Snow-White and Rose-Red**
Retold by Antonia Barber    Illustrated by Gilly Marklew

**Sleeping Beauty**
Retold by Ann Turnbull    Illustrated by Sophy Williams

**Rumpelstiltskin**
Retold by Helen Cresswell    Illustrated by John Howe

**Goldilocks and the Three Bears**
Retold by Penelope Lively    Illustrated by Debi Gliori

PRINTED IN BELGIUM BY

INTERNATIONAL BOOK PRODUCTION